TALKING IS NOT MY THING

ROSE ROBBINS is the author of *Me and My Sister* (Eerdmans), a companion to *Talking Is Not My Thing*. She has a master of arts in children's book illustration from the Cambridge School of Art and was a runner-up for Hachette UK's Carmelite Prize in 2017. Rose grew up with an autistic brother, an experience that informs and shapes her writing. She serves as an ambassador with Inclusive Minds, an organization that promotes quality representation in children's literature, and she has written and drawn extensively about neurodiversity issues. Rose lives in Nottingham, UK. Follow her on Instagram @roserobbinsuk and visit her website at roserobbins.co.uk.

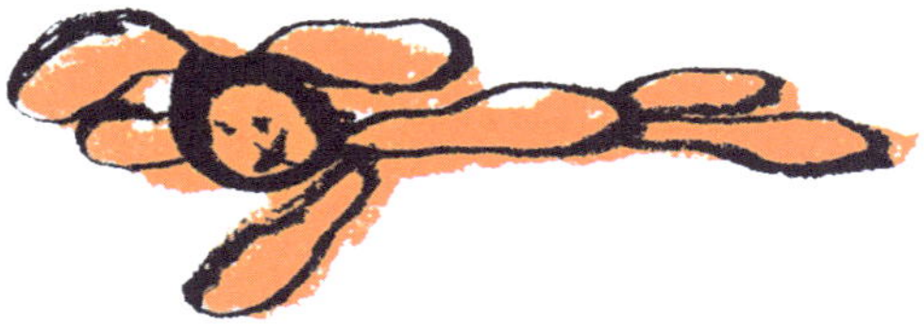

For Rowland

ACKNOWLEDGMENTS

I owe an extraordinary debt to the people whom I have approached for guidance while writing this book: Lilo, Frances, and Carly. In particular, I would like to thank Dr. Rebecca Butler for her continual advice and support throughout the production of this book.

— R. R.

First published in the United States in 2020
by Eerdmans Books for Young Readers,
an imprint of Wm. B. Eerdmans Publishing Co.
Grand Rapids, Michigan

www.eerdmans.com/youngreaders

First published in Great Britain in 2020
by Scallywag Press Ltd., London

Manufactured in China

29 28 27 26 25 24 23 22 21 20 1 2 3 4 5 6 7 8 9

Library of Congress Cataloging-in-Publication Data

Names: Robbins, Rose, author.
Title: Talking is not my thing / Rose Robbins.
Description: Grand Rapids : Eerdmans Books for Young Readers, [2020] | Audience: Ages 3-7. | Summary: A girl with autism who almost never speaks demonstrates how easily she communicates with her brother and grandmother through facial expressions, gestures, flashcards, and drawings.
Identifiers: LCCN 2020000612 | ISBN 9780802855497 (hardcover)
Subjects: CYAC: Selective mutism—Fiction. | Brothers and sisters—Fiction. | Autism—Fiction.
Classification: LCC PZ7.1.R583 Tal 2020 | DDC [E]—dc23
LC record available at https://lccn.loc.gov/2020000612

TALKING IS NOT MY THING

ROSE ROBBINS

EERDMANS BOOKS FOR YOUNG READERS • GRAND RAPIDS, MICHIGAN

I don't speak. But my brother finds it easy!

COME INSIDE! IT'S NEARLY DINNER.

I hope
we are having
spaghetti!

I THINK WE ARE HAVING SPAGHETTI!

Sometimes I try to use my voice...

But the words don't come out right.
EEP?

All the noises at dinner are too much. I wish I could turn my ears off.

But I still like to feel included.
THAT WAS YUMMY! LET'S GO AND WATCH TV WITH GRANDMA!

THESE PLANTS NEED LOTS OF WATER!
hmm... I think I need one of my flashcards!

DO YOU WANT TO GO TO THE TOILET, DEAR?
yes!

FLUSH
Sometimes I need a bit of help when I have to go.
ALL DONE!

I am teaching my brother a guessing game with drawing...

He is getting quite good at it!
PURPLE TURTLE!

I love books! My brother is going to read to me...

Look! It's 7 o'clock!
TIME TO BRUSH OUR TEETH!

My toothbrush is easy to find – it looks like a DRAGON!

BRUSH
BRUSH
BRUSH

Time to put my pajamas on...

Oh! Where's Bunny?

EEEEEEEEEEE!
WHERE ARE YOU GOING NOW?

IT'S DARK OUTSIDE! WAIT FOR ME!
Where is she?

HEY! IS THAT WHAT YOU WERE LOOKING FOR?

There she is!

I'm so glad to have Bunny back again.
We do a happy dance...

... until it's
time for bed.

OUCH!
HEE HEE!

OH WOW! YOU FOUND MY CAR.

High five!
HIGH FIVE!